Let's Own Up

By Janine Amos and Annabel Spenceley

Consultant Rachael Underwood

an imprint of
WINDMILL BOOKS
New York

Published in the United States by Alphabet Soup, an imprint of Windmill Books, LLC

Windmill Books
303 Park Avenue South
Suite #1280
New York, NY 10010

Library of Congress Cataloging-in-Publication Data

Amos, Janine
    Let's own up. – 1st North American ed. / by Janine Amos and Annabel Spenceley.
cm. – (Best behavior)
    Contents: Alice and Dad—Building models.
    Summary: Two brief stories demonstrate the importance of admitting our mistakes
and working together to make things better.
    ISBN 978-1-60754-503-3 (lib.) – 978-1-60754-505-7 (pbk.)
978-1-60754-506-4 (6 pack)
    1. Truthfulness and falsehood—Juvenile literature   [1. Honesty
2. Conduct of life]   I. Spenceley, Annabel   II. Title   III. Series
    177/.1—dc22

Manufactured in China

With thanks to: Nicholas and Alice Turpin, Edward Evans, and Nahal Rao

Alice and Dad

The kitchen's
a mess.

4

Dad cleans
it up.

He washes the dishes.
He cleans the floor.

He clears the table.
He throws all the
trash away.

Alice comes in. "Where's my model?" she asks. "It was on the table."

Dad looks at Alice.
He looks at the waste basket.

"I made a mistake, Alice,"
says Dad. "I put your model
in the waste basket."

Alice is upset.
Her dad gives
her a hug.

"I'm sorry," says Dad.
"That model was important
to you, wasn't it?"

Alice nods her head.
How does she feel?

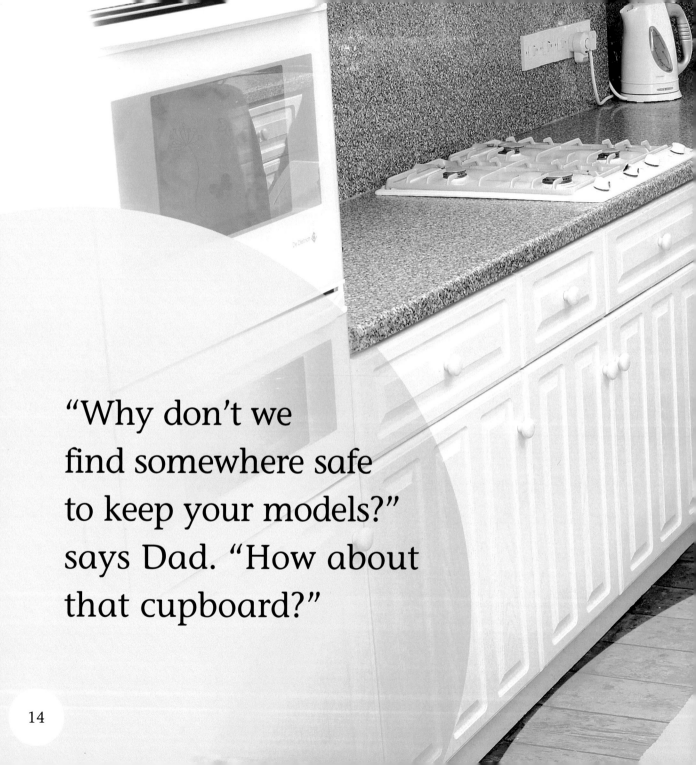

"Why don't we
find somewhere safe
to keep your models?"
says Dad. "How about
that cupboard?"

"Yes!" agrees Alice.
"We'll need to empty
it first," Dad tells her.

"Let's do it now!" says Alice.
"OK," says Dad.

Alice makes another model.

And then Dad cleans up the kitchen again!

Building Models

"Chug! Chug! I'm building
a tractor," says Edward.

Edward works hard. The tractor is finished. He looks in the box for a driver.

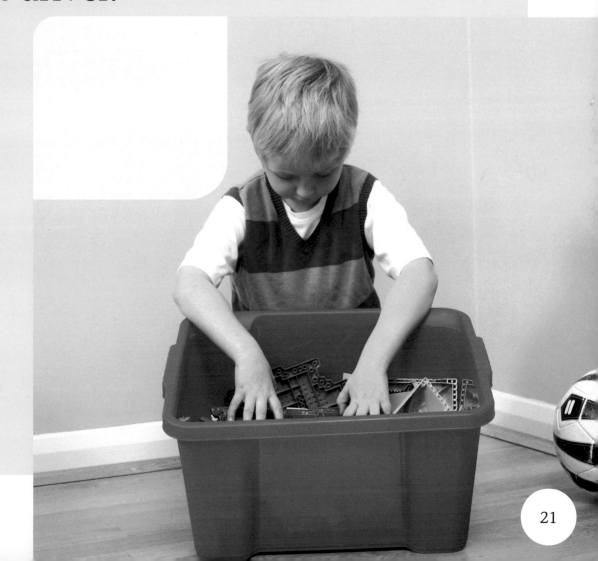

Nahal comes to build a train.

He picks up Edward's tractor and
pulls it apart. He uses the tractor
to make his train.

"Hey! Where's my tractor?"
Edward asks.
"I used it in my train," says Nahal.
"I didn't know."

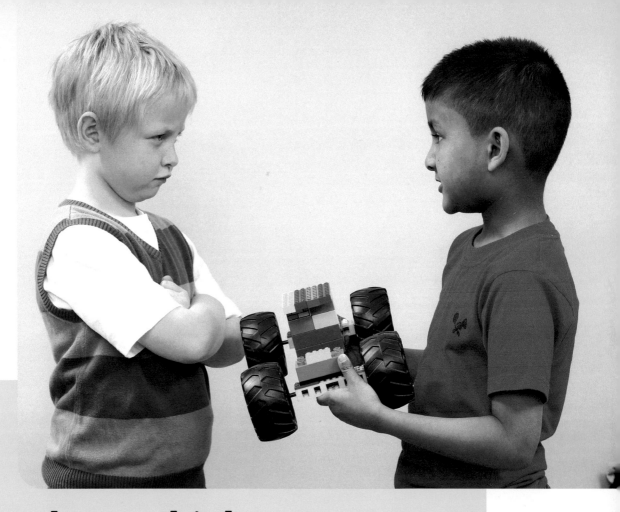

How do you think
Edward feels?
How does Nahal feel?
What could they do?

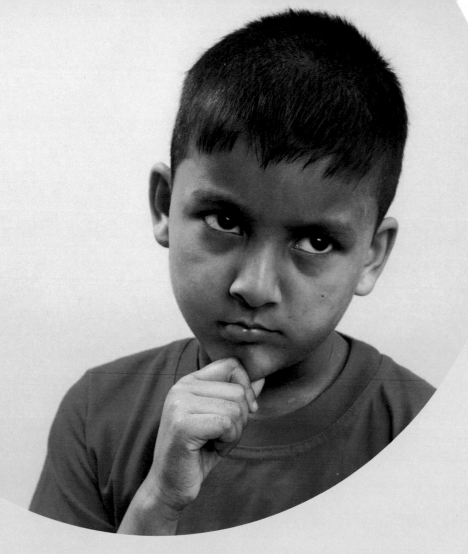

Nahal thinks hard.
"You can play with
my train," he says.

"But I want a tractor,"
Edward tells him.

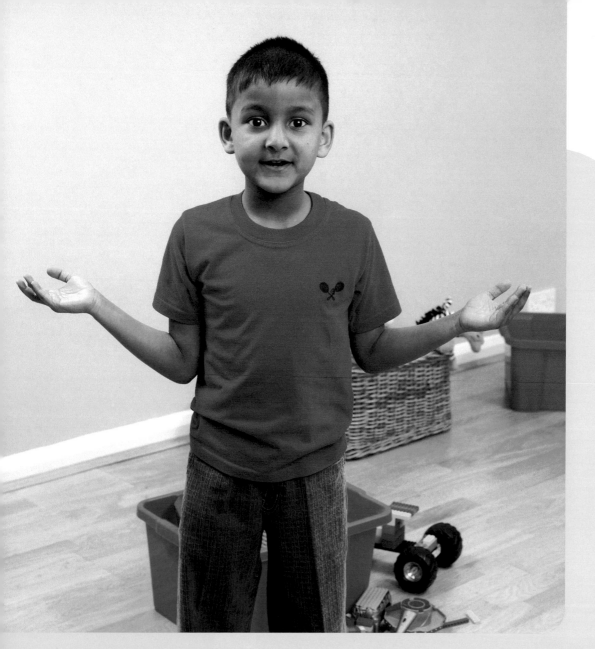

"What should we do?" asks Nahal.

"We could make this into a new tractor," says Edward.

"Yes — with great big wheels!" agrees Nahal.

Together they build a new tractor.

FOR FURTHER READING

INFORMATION BOOKS
Burch, Regina. *Telling the Truth: Learning About Honesty, Integrity, and Trustworhiness*. Huntington Beach, CA: Creative Teaching Press, 2002.

Meiners, Cheri J. *Be Honest and Tell the Truth*. Minneapolis: Free Spirit Publishing, 2007.

FICTION
Barkan, Joanne. *The Boy Who Cried Wolf: A Tale About Telling the Truth*. New York: Reader's Digest Young Families, 2006.

Braver, Vanita. *Pinky Promise: A Book About Telling the Truth*. Washington: Child & Family Press, 2004.

AUTHOR BIO
Janine Amos has worked in publishing as an editor and author, and as a lecturer in education. Her interests are in personal growth and raising self-esteem, and she works with educators, child psychologists, and specialists in mediation. She has written more than fifty books for children. Many of her titles deal with first-time experiences and emotional health issues such as bullying, death, and divorce.

You can find more great fiction and nonfiction from Windmill Books at windmillbooks.com